We're Going to Have a Baby

Doris Wild Helmering
John William Helmering

illustrated by
Robert H. Cassell

ABINGDON
Nashville

We're Going to Have a Baby

Copyright © 1978 by Doris Wild Helmering and
John William Helmering

Printed in the United States of America

Library of Congress Cataloging in Publication Data
Helmering, Doris Wild, 1942–
    We're going to have a baby.

    SUMMARY: Jimmy is glad there's going to be a new baby in his
family until his friend advises him babies are nothing to be happy about.
    [1. Brothers and sisters—Fiction] I. Helmering, John, 1965–
joint author. II. Title.
PZ7.H3758We   [E]   77-24742

ISBN 0-687-44446-2

To
Dad and Paul
and
The Lamping Family

Hi.
My name is Jimmy. I'm four years old.

Last night at the dinner table my mom and dad told me a secret. Well, it was my dad who told me. He had a big smile on his face, and he told me that we are going to have a baby! Right now the baby is growing in my mother's body.

I figured something was going to happen in our family. You see, sometimes when we are all watching television, I sit on my mother's lap. Well, lately she hasn't had much room for me on her lap.

And, too, there is a bedroom next to mine that nobody ever uses. It holds all the family junk, like old lamps and furniture, as well as clothes and broken toys that need to be fixed.

Last week all the junk had been cleaned out. The room was very "nice and tidy," as my mom would say. And my old white crib was in the room.

And one thing for sure—I couldn't fit in that white crib anymore!

So now I know. We are going to have a baby. My mother can't fit me on her lap anymore because there is a baby that fills up her lap. And the junk room has been cleaned up for the baby.

I smiled when my dad and mom first told me we were going to have a baby. They were both smiling, and they looked very happy. So I was happy too.

I could play trucks with the baby and stack blocks and color books and play dolls. And when it rained, I would have a friend to play with right in my very own house. Having a baby is going to be fun.

That evening after dinner, I went to Joe's
house to tell him the good news. Joe is six,
and he lives down the street from me. I
said, "Guess what, Joe." But Joe couldn't
guess. So I told him, "We are going to have
a baby."

When Joe heard my secret, he didn't smile like my mom and dad had smiled. He just sat on the steps and frowned.

Joe is older, and I figured that he must know something about a baby that I didn't know. Besides, last year Joe got a baby sister. So I said, "Come on, Joe, tell me, what's the matter with a baby?"

And, oh boy, Joe sure told me what was the matter. He said that babies scream and cry a lot. They cry if they are hungry. They cry if they want their diaper changed. They cry if they want to be picked up—cry, cry, cry. Where could we go to watch television with all that crying?

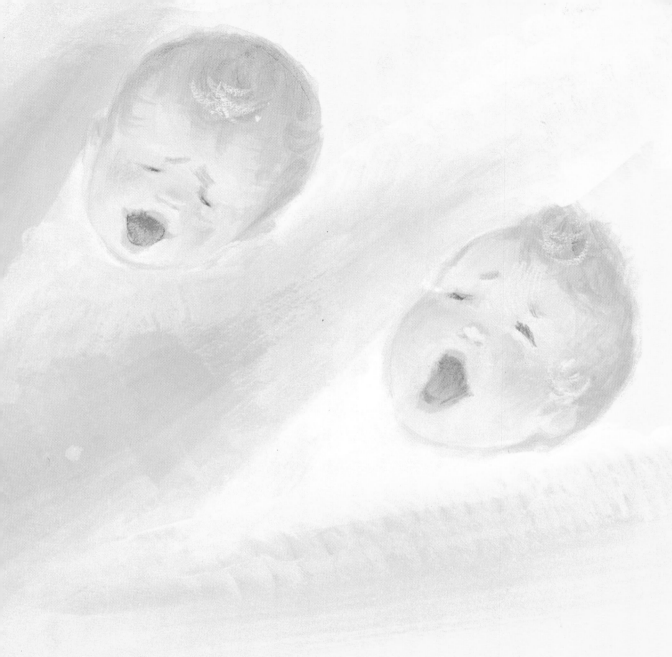

He also told me that when babies start to crawl around on the floor, life gets worse! You can't leave any of your building blocks or models or books around because a baby will eat anything. So having a baby would be no fun.

"A baby can't feed itself or go to the bathroom by itself," Joe told me, "and you know what that means—your mom and dad will be very busy with that baby."

I told Joe good-bye and went home to figure things out because now I was really mixed up.

Mom and Dad were GLAD about the baby.

Joe was MAD about the baby.

And, all of a sudden, I didn't feel glad anymore. I felt SCARED.

What if Joe was right? What if the baby was always crying, and I couldn't hear my favorite television show? What if the baby was always eating or going to the bathroom in its pants? What if Mom and Dad didn't have any time for me? I wouldn't like that!

When I got home my dad and mom were doing the dishes; so I sat in the kitchen and drank a glass of milk. I listened very carefully to them talking about the baby. Yep, no doubt about it. They were feeling glad.

The next day after I woke up, I took another look at the baby's room and wondered if Joe were right. Would the baby always be crying? Would the baby eat my toys?

I ate my breakfast and then went outside to play. First I played with Mr. Barker. That's my dog. But he wasn't very much fun. So then I sat down in my sandbox and started making a picture. But that wasn't much fun either. I just kept thinking about the baby.

All of a sudden a big tear rolled down my
face. I opened my mouth and caught it with
my tongue. Then another tear ran down my
face. Soon I had so many tears rolling down
my face that I just couldn't catch them all. I
was crying, and I felt really SAD.

About that time, Mr. Bond, the man who lives next door, walked out into his yard and started trimming his roses. He has a rose garden right next to the fence. On the other side of the fence is my sandbox.

Of course, he saw me crying, and so he asked, "Why are you so sad, Jimmy?" I told him that we were going to have a new baby and that I had felt GLAD. But Joe had felt MAD, and then I felt SCARED. Now I felt SAD. I was really mixed up.

Mr. Bond smiled and said he didn't think that I was mixed up at all. He said it was all right for me to have all those feelings about the baby's coming.

He said I would probably feel MAD sometimes—especially if the baby messed up my toys and chewed on my nice books.

He said I might even feel SCARED that maybe my mom and dad might love the baby more than they loved me. But they would really love me too.

He said I might feel SAD sometimes when my mom and dad were busy with the baby and I wanted them to pay attention to me. I might have to share my mom and dad.

But I would feel GLAD because having a new baby would be a real adventure. Mr. Bond said, "Babies are tiny, and they can't do much at first. But in a couple of months the baby will begin to smile at you. And one day the baby will be able to say your name, Jimmy." I laughed at that.

Mr. Bond told me that the baby would probably get into my toys at times, but I could teach the baby not to break things. Mr. Bond told me I would be the baby's teacher. I could help the baby learn new words and help the baby walk.

But best of all, I would be the baby's big brother. And one thing I know—a baby loves its big brother.

Yeah! Mr. Bond was right. I could have all those feelings—I could be SCARED, MAD, SAD, and GLAD. But all those feelings are okay. And that's how it is when you are going to have a new baby in your house.